The Xmas

Factor

First published 2012 by A & C Black,
an imprint of Bloomsbury Publishing Plc
50 Bedford Square
London WC1B 3DP

www.bloomsbury.com

Copyright © 2012 A & C Black
Text copyright © 2012 Jonathan Meres
Illustrations copyright © 2012 Nikalas Catlow

The right of Jonathan Meres and Nikalas Catlow to be identified as the author
and illustrator of this work has been asserted by them in accordance with the
Copyrights, Designs and Patents Act 1988.

ISBN 978-1-4081-8033-4

A CIP catalogue for this book is available from the British Library.

MIX
Paper from
responsible sources
FSC® C020471

Printed and Bound by CPI Group (UK) Ltd, Croydon CR0 4YY

1 3 5 7 9 10 8 6 4 2

The Xmas Factor

Jonathan Meres

No turkeys were harmed during the writing of this book.

A & C BLACK
AN IMPRINT OF BLOOMSBURY
LONDON   NEW DELHI   NEW YORK   SYDNEY

I'm dreaming of a quiet Christmas
Like none I've ever known before
Where noise is banned throughout the land
And wearing loud shirts is against the law
I'm dreaming of a quiet Christmas
One spent all day tucked up in bed
Where carol singers and sleigh bell ringers
Stay home and play Monopoly instead
I'm dreaming of a quiet Christmas
Where kids wake up just after noon
Is being unseasonable so unreasonable?
Can't help wishing it was June.

A turkey's not for life – it's just for Christmas.*

* Only joking.**

** You can eat a turkey anytime.

Fairy: Doctor, doctor, I've got terrible tummy ache.

Doctor: I'm not surprised. You've got a Christmas tree stuck up your bum.

**What do you call a reindeer
with no eyes?**
A rendeer.

**What do you call a reindeer
with no ears?**
Anything you like. It can't hear you.

**What did Mrs
Claus say to Santa
when she looked
out the window?**
"Looks like reindeer."

Did you hear about the snowman who couldn't spell?
He had a parrot for a nose.

(He couldn't smell either.)

What song do snowmen sing when it's another snowman's birthday?
Freeze a jolly good fellow.

What do Rudolph the Red-Nosed Reindeer and Frosty the Snowman have in common?
They both have the same middle name.

IT'S A CRACKING CHRISTMAS FACT...

...that tinsel was invented by a man from Oldham in Greater Manchester called Barry Tinsel. It's thought he got the idea when he witnessed a squirrel getting its tail stuck in an electric socket.*

* Don't try that at home**, kids.

** Or anywhere, for that matter.

...that instead of hanging stockings under the chimney, in some countries children hang pants. Not their own pants. Their mum's pants. (Because they hold more.)

...that during the festive period, Chocolate Oranges count towards your 5-a-day.

SINGALONGACHRISTMAS

Jingle bells
Various smells
Make me want to heave
Dinner's started, Grandma's farted
Think it's time to leave.

Christmas is coming, the goose is on a diet
If someone touches my mince pies there's gonna
be a riot.

Christmas is coming, the goose
is getting thinner
If there's a prize for eating pies
there'll only be
one winner.

Christmas is coming, the goose
has disappeared
But so it seems have all the
pies — how very, very weird.

PIE NEWS

We're getting reports that Santa Claus is coming to town. Members of the public have been advised that they'd better watch out and that they'd better not cry. Not only is Santa making a list, he's checking it twice in order to find out just who's naughty and who's nice. A spokesman for the town claims that not only does Santa know when you're sleeping, he also knows when you're awake, and that it's therefore in everybody's best interests to be good for goodness sake.

BREAKING NEWS • BREAKING NEWS • BREAKING NEWS

TOP CHRISTMAS TIPS...

🌲 Wise man travelling from the East? Don't forget to put your clocks back!

🌲 Instead of staring gormlessly at the TV all day, why not talk* to each other instead?

*Talking was a popular pastime in the 1970s as well as an effective method of communication, but has been steadily declining ever since.

🌲 Instead of eating all the nuts and oranges at the bottom of your stocking, why not put them back in the bowl again till next year?

CHRISTMAS TRADITIONS

Who was the first person to decorate a tree? Why do we deck the halls with boughs of holly and not sticks of celery? Traditions have to begin somewhere – so why not make up some of your own? Here are some suggestions to get you started:

- Celebrate the first day of December by running round your garden completely naked, shouting "Christmas is coming! Christmas is coming!"

- Nail a sprout to your front door in order to keep evil spirits at bay.

- Smear turkey fat on the faces of any visitors over the festive period.

- Eat nothing but baked beans on December 8th.

- Spend the whole of December 9th on the toilet.

SANTA'S POSTBAG

Dere Santer

Four krismus this yere pleze may I hav a dikshunry?

From Charlie age 8

Dear Santa

This year for Christmas I would like peace and happiness throughout the world. And goodwill to all men. And women. And a bike.

Thank you from Rachel

Should be made illegal

Produce gas

Really pongy gas

Other vegetables are available

Under no circumstances should you ever eat them

Take your life in your hands if you do

Silent but deadly

....that the total amount of gas produced by eating sprouts over the Christmas period is enough to power a country the size of Wales.*

*The trouble is – no one would want to live there.

...that if all the mince pies in the world were laid end to end... that would be really stupid. And a terrible waste of pies.

...that in some states of the USA it's illegal to eat a mince pie before December 1st.

Grandpa: When I was your age we made our own entertainment.
Kid: Really, Grandpa? You *made* an Xbox?

Did you hear about the kid who loved sprouts?
Me neither.

What's the difference between Santa Claus and a banana?
One's a jolly old elf who flies round the world delivering toys to children – and the other is a kind of fruit.

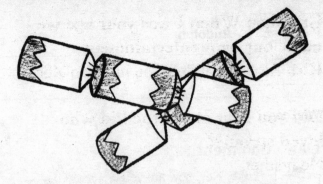

Why was the Christmas cracker joke not funny?
Because it was past its tell-by date.

I got a scarf for Christmas.
I had to take it back because it was too tight.

Knock, knock.
Who's there?
Santa. There's no chimney.

My snowman's got no nose.
How does it smell?
It doesn't.

Rudolph

24 December

Who nose?

Like • Comment

 Frosty Hey, how are you?

 Rudolph Fed up. You?

 Frosty Just chilling. What's up?

 Rudolph All of the other reindeer.

 Frosty What about them?

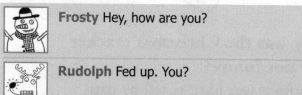 **Rudolph** They keep laughing and calling me names.

Frosty Just because you've got a red nose?

18

Rudolph Yeah. And now they won't let me join in any reindeer games.

 Santa Ho, ho, ho.

 Santa What are you doing later, Rudy?

 Rudolph Nothing much. Why?

 Santa It's getting foggy and I was wondering whether you'd mind helping pull my sleigh?

 Rudolph Seriously?

 Santa Absolutely.

 Rudolph Cool!!!

 Frosty Reindeer games are pretty rubbish anyway.

YOU'RE NOT THE REAL SANTA

You're not the real Santa
Your beard is clearly fake
Your bum's too small, you're much too tall
You're thinner than a rake.

You're not the real Santa
There's nothing in that sack
Your ho-ho's only so-so
You can have your present back.

You're not the real Santa
You must think that I'm mad
Your knee's too bony, you're
   a phony
Admit it, you're my dad.

y couldn't Santa do any gardening?

l lost his hoe-hoe-hoe.

you hear about Santa trying his
d at stand-up comedy?

sleighed 'em.

ck, knock.
o's there?
a.
a who?
at do you mean,
a who? Are you
id or
ething?

PIE NEWS

A man is being questioned by police on suspicion of not being the real Santa Claus. The man was discovered in a department store earlier today, with a queue of children waiting to see him and tell him what they wanted for Christmas in exchange for a small gift. A number of people dressed as elves are also helping police with their enquiries.

IT'S A CRACKING CHRISTMAS FACT...

...that the chances of turkeys taking over the world and wreaking revenge on humankind are actually very slim indeed. Phew!

...that it isn't actually the same robin you see posing on all those Christmas cards. There are many different robins.

...that in some countries the most popular creature featured on Christmas cards isn't a robin at all but a badger.

I'D LIKE TO BE A CHRISTMAS FAIRY

I'd like to be a Christmas fairy
Sitting on a tree
A fairy on a Christmas tree
Is what I'd like to be.

You can keep your Eiffel Tower
And your Himalayas too
A stocking stuffed with sweets and toys
Is what I call a view.

I'd like to be a Christmas fairy
Taking in the sights
The only problem seems to be
That I am scared of heights.

Why was Santa's shortest helper unhappy?
He had low elf-esteem.

Why was Santa's helper not allowed to ride in the sleigh?
Elf and safety.

Did you hear about Santa's Superstore?
It was elf-service.

Why did Santa have to tell one of his helpers off?
For being too elf-centred.

COOKING TIPS

Vegetarian? Still want to experience a traditional Christmas lunch? Tough luck. You can't.*

* Only joking of course. Simply carve a load of mashed potato into the shape of a turkey. Colour it by covering in brown sauce.**

** Then have cold mashed potato sandwiches for the next three days.***

*** And mashed potato curry after that.

Looking for the best way to cook sprouts? Look no further!

1. Take 100g of sprouts.

2. Wash them.

3. Peel and throw excess leaves in bin.

4. Throw the rest of the sprouts in the bin too.

THE XMAS FILES

Name:	Santa Claus
AKA:	Father Christmas, St Nick
Job title:	Seasonal Parcel Distribution Executive
Favourite colour:	Beige. (Just kidding. It's red, really.)
Hobbies:	Going to the gym (Again – just kidding.)
Likes:	Sleeping
Dislikes:	Shaving
Favourite word:	Ho
Least favourite word:	Nomoremincepies

PIE NEWS

Fire services have been tackling a blaze at a house. There are no reports of any casualties. Early reports indicate that one possible cause is chestnuts roasting on an open fire. A spokesman has warned that chestnuts should only ever be roasted on an open fire under strict adult supervision and should never be left unattended under any circumstances, whether Jack Frost is nipping on your nose, Yuletide carols are being sung by a choir, or Santa's on his way. Wherever possible, an alternative method of cooking chestnuts should be used, such as microwaving, or heating in an oven at 180 degrees for approximately 15 minutes, turning half way through.

Doctor, doctor, I've swallowed some Christmas decorations.
You've got tinselitis.

Doctor, doctor, I keep thinking I'm a Christmas tree.
Go and stand in the corner.

Doctor, doctor, I keep hearing jingle bells.
Ring for an appointment.

Doctor, doctor, I keep thinking I'm a set of fairy lights.
Switch yourself off on the way out.

CHRISTMAS TOP TIPS

🌲 Why not use unwanted jumpers and scarves that your grandma's knitted as loft insulation? An effectively insulated loft can reduce energy bills by as much as 53%.*

* According to research that I've just made up.

🌲 Why not ask your gran to knit you something *really* useful this Christmas? Like money.

🌲 Worried about trees being needlessly cut down for the Christmas period, then discarded a couple of weeks later? Why not decorate a clothes-horse or a chair instead?

IT'S A CRACKING CHRISTMAS FACT...

...that the first Christmas crackers traditionally contained not only a hilarious Victorian joke*, but a tiny map of Belgium and a small portion of cheese.

> *
>
> *How many Victorians does it take to change a light bulb?*
>
> *None. Light bulbs haven't been invented yet.*

...that 100g of sprouts have exactly the same nutritional value as a small piece of cardboard. But they're not quite as tasty.

How many snowmen does it take to change a lightbulb?

Under no circumstances should a snowman ever attempt to change a lightbulb. If they really need to change one, they should contact a qualified electrician. Or at least someone with arms and who isn't made of frozen water.

This joke was brought to you by The Royal Society for Prevention of Accidents to Snowmen.

What did the snowman have for breakfast?

Frosties.

What did one Christmas tree sing to another Christmas tree on its birthday?

Fir tree's a jolly good fellow.

Why did the turkey cross the road?
It was following the chicken.

Why couldn't the turkey eat any more?
It was stuffed.

What did the turkey say when it got too hot?
"I'm absolutely roasting. Can someone open the door?"

SANTA'S POSTBAG

Dear Santa

Thanks very much for the slippers, the socks and the talcum powder you brought me last Christmas. This year please can I have some proper presents?

From Steven (7¼)

Dear Mr Claus, or may I call you Santa?

I appreciate that you must be very busy at the moment with Christmas coming up, but if you have time do you think I could possibly have some Lego? I collect a little bit every year. I'm saving up to build a house. A real house. I may be some time.

Sincerely

Callum, aged 3,334 days

SINGALONGACHRISTMAS

While shepherds watched their
   clocks by night

All seated on the ground

Some robbers came and
   nicked their sheep

And still they've* not
   been found.

*The sheep – not the robbers.

We three kings of Orient are

Bearing gifts we traverse afar

Would've got here sooner

But honestly you should've seen the traffic.

Fifi the Fairy

24 December

I am SO FED UP!!!!

Like • Comment

Rudolph What's up, grumpy knickers?

Fifi Wouldn't you be grumpy sat on top of a tree all day?

Rudolph Fairy nuff.

Fifi You trying to be funny?

Rudolph Sorry. Won't happen again.

Fifi I don't even like trees. They bring me out in a rash. And I'm scared of heights.

Rudolph Tell me about it.

Fifi You're scared of heights?

 Rudolph Not just scared. Petrified.

 Fifi But you're a flying reindeer!

 Rudolph I know! What am I like, eh?

 Santa Oi! Rudy! You coming tonight, or what?

 Rudolph We need to talk, boss.

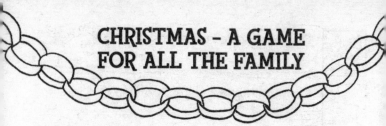

CHRISTMAS – A GAME FOR ALL THE FAMILY

Aim: To remind everyone just how much they hate playing board games and how they'd much rather be doing something else instead. Anything. It really doesn't matter what.

Instructions:

1. Roll dice to see who begins.

2. Argue about who got the highest.

3. Let youngest begin anyway so he/she doesn't go off in a huff.

4. Wake Grandma.

5. Immediately start bickering. Preferably about something really trivial and unimportant – but which quickly escalates until frankly there's a bit of an atmosphere.

6. Someone lets off a right old stinker and blames the dog.

7. Realise you don't actually have a dog. Blame Grandma instead.

8. Listen to lecture about how there were no such things as computers in the olden days and how people had to make their own entertainment.

9. Go to toilet and check Facebook. Preferably not at same time.

10. Wake Grandma again.

11. Give up.

The winner is the first person to switch the telly on.

...that the inventor of the Christmas cracker got the idea for the 'cracking' sound when he heard the noise that a log makes when it's thrown on a fire. Good job he didn't get it when he was passing the toilet.

...that in some countries it's traditional to not decorate your tree until the first star is visible on Christmas Eve. If it's cloudy, Christmas can be cancelled altogether.

...that if someone tells you they really don't want anything for Christmas this year... THEY'RE LYING!!!

40

SINGALONGACHRISTMAS

Good King Wenceslas looked out
On the feast of Stephen
There was no snow whatsoever
That's global warming for you.*

* It turned out it was actually the warmest
feast of Stephen since records began.

We three kings of Orient are
Having problems with our car
One three king just phoned ahead
To say we're on the train instead.

THIS POEM HAS NOTHING TO DO WITH CHRISTMAS

There are no reindeer in this poem
No non-stop elves forever on the go
This poem has no stockings hung with care in it
This poem has no walking in the air in it
This poem has nothing to do with Christmas.

There are no mince pies in this poem
No references to shepherds, sheep, or snow
This poem has no hyper girls or boys in it
This poem has no mistletoe or toys in it
This poem has nothing to do with Christmas.

There are no turkeys in this poem
No Santa dressed in red from head to toe
There's a distinct dearth of mirth in it
There's a lack of peace on
    earth in it
This poem was written in April.

TOP CHRISTMAS TIPS

🎄 When given a present that you don't really want, never blurt out, "Have you got the receipt?" straight away. Wait at least five minutes.

🎄 Never eat yellow snow.

🎄 Scare off unwanted carol singers* by answering the door dressed as the ghost of a turkey.

*That's singers of carols, by the way. Not singers called Carol.

What do you call a snowman made out of flour*?

Frosty the Doughman.

* Not strictly a snowman, then.

Did you hear about Santa losing his job?

He got the sack.

What do you call Santa with no pants?

Saint Knickerless.

What do you call a sick reindeer?
Spewdolph.

**What do you call a cow crossed
with a reindeer?**
Moodolph.

**Why didn't the three wise men
have smelly feet?**
Because the shepherds washed their
socks by night.

THE XMAS FILES

Name:	Frosty
Occupation:	Snowman
Hobbies:	Walking in the air
Likes:	Chilling
Dislikes:	Carrots
Favourite food:	Nothing too hot
Favourite word:	Cool
Least favourite word:	Uncool

STOCKING FILLERS

I'd like to be a snowman
I'd like to stand and stare
I'd watch the world go by
Instead of walking in the air.

Mince pie with my little eye
Something beginning with 'Y'
Yum.

CHRISTMAS (W)RAP

Let me hear you say ho
Let me hear you say ho, ho
Let me hear you say ho, ho ho.

PIE NEWS

A man has been rescued after getting stuck up a chimney. A passer-by is believed to have discovered the man when he heard him shout, "You girls and boys won't get any toys if you don't pull me out!" Emergency services were called to the scene. According to a spokesman, not only was the man's beard black, but there was soot in his sack and his nose was tickly too.

SANTA'S POSTBAG

Dear Santa

Please may I have a new brother for Christmas? The one I've got at the moment is rubbish.
Thank you.

Chloe aged 8½

Dear Santa

Thank you very much for the remote control car, the keyboard and the torch you brought me last year. This year, I would like some batteries.

From Robert aged 8

'TWAS THE NIGHT AFTER CHRISTMAS

'Twas the night after Christmas and all through
the flat

Not a creature was stirring, not even the cat.

The plates in the sink had been chucked
without care

In the hope that the dish-fairy soon would be there,

When out of the lounge there arose such a sound

I sprang out of bed without touching the ground.

My dad in his armchair was snoring his head off

Whilst letting out farts which would frighten the
dead off.

The smell was horrendous, part parsnip, part sprout:

I opened the window to let it all out.

I tried to be quiet but despite my intention

He woke with some language I'd better not mention.

But he said as I tiptoed and
turned out the light

Merry Christmas to all and
to all – a goodnight.

...that due to global warming, Santa is being forced to relocate his workshop from Lapland* to an industrial estate just outside Birmingham.

* Lapland is actually where laptops were invented.**

** Not really.

Ding dong merrily on high, goes the popular Christmas carol. But just how high? The highest ever ding dong recorded was 2.73 metres, by James Dukes, in Bumfluff, Illinois, on 23rd December 1973.

...that in some* countries, Christmas decorations remain up for most of the year and only actually get taken down for their so-called '12 Undays of Christmas.'

* Completely made-up countries, such as Mundania, Costa Fortuna and Rebeccastan.

**Doctor, doctor, I keep thinking
I'm a candle.**
Better not go out.

**Doctor, doctor, I keep thinking I'm
a Christmas present.**
You'd better keep it under wraps.

**Doctor, doctor, I keep thinking I'm a
Christmas cracker.**
Pull the other one.

**Doctor, doctor, I keep
thinking I'm a turkey.**
You're talking gobbledygook.

COOKING TIPS

Want to know how to
make Christmashed
Potatoes? Simple! Just
make ordinary mashed
potatoes, and stick
a bit of tinsel on top!

Want to know how to make Christmushy Peas?
Simple! Take some peas, mush them up, and stick a
bit of tinsel on top!

Want to know how to make a Yule Log? Simple!
Get an ordinary log and stick a bit of tinsel on top!
Delicious with custard.

STOCKING FILLERS

When January first appeared
Santa Claus shaved off his beard
It seems he did it for a bet
And no one's recognised him yet.

Santa
Drank a Fanta
This fact is unassailable
Other drinks are available.

I punctured my bicycle
On an icicle
It was not nicicle.

PIE NEWS

Santa Claus has been fined for speeding. According to a police spokesman, not only was Santa dashing through the snow on a one-horse open sleigh, he was doing so at 35 mph in a 30 mph area and laughing all the way. Said the spokesman, "To break the speed limit was one thing, but all that ho-ho-hoing was just taking the mickey."

What do you call Santa when he's in the shower?
Lather Christmas.

What do you get when you cross a snowman with James Bond?
A license to chill.

A log's not for life
It's just for Christmas.

Doctor, doctor, I keep wanting to sit on top of a Christmas tree.
You're a star.

IT'S A CRACKING CHRISTMAS FACT...

...that reindeers weren't Santa's first choice of creatures to pull his sleigh. His first choice was actually cows – based entirely on their ability to jump over the moon. Fortunately* someone pointed out that this actually only happens in nursery rhymes.

*Well, you wouldn't want to be underneath a sleigh pulled by flying cows, would you?

...that in some parts of South America, turkeys are worshipped as gods and allowed to wander about and do exactly as they please. At least until Christmas, when they're all rounded up and eaten.

CHRISTMAS TOP TIPS

🌲 Use unwanted* sprouts as weapons. Wait till Grandpa's fallen asleep and then use his open mouth for target practice.**

* That's basically all sprouts then.

** Just joking. Really not a good idea at all.***

*** Use grapes instead.

🌲 Decked the hall with boughs of holly, and still got some holly left over? Why not deck the rest of the house, too?

🌲 Dreaming of a green Christmas? Why not recycle old cracker jokes by using them year after year after year?

SINGALONGACHRISTMAS

I saw Mommy texting Santa Claus
Underneath the mistletoe just now
She didn't seem to see
Me on the way back from a pee
She thought that I was in my bedroom playing
   on my Wii.

I saw three sheep come sailing in
What a weird dream that was!

Good King Wenceslas
   looked out
on the feast of Stephen
nothing much was
   happening
everyone was leaving.

Dear Santa,

Don't listen to my mum. I've been really good this year. Honest. It wasn't my fault my brother tripped and hit my fist with his nose. And I didn't mean to break that teapot. Anyway I don't know what the big deal was. Mum said it belonged to her Grandma. So it's about time she got a new one. Please can I have a laptop? The dog peed on my old one. Hope you're well.

All the best

Marlon (nearly 10)

Elvis the Elf

24 December

Busy, busy and more busy.

Like • Comment

Frosty Obviously not that busy then?

Elvis Why do you say that?

Frosty Well you're on Facebook, aren't you?

Elvis I'M ON A BREAK!!!!!

Frosty All right, all right. Keep your hair on!

Elvis At least I've got some, Carrot nose!

Frosty No need to get personal.

Elvis Sorry. I'm a bit stressed.

 Frosty Forget about it.

 Elvis Are we cool?

 Frosty Well I don't know about you but I'm very cool!

 Elvis LOL

THE XMAS FILES

Name: Elvis

Position: Elf – and if you honestly think I've got time to answer your ridiculous questions you've got another think coming!!!

CHRISTMAS TOP TIPS

 Fed up listening to your little brother moaning about some stupid toy that doesn't work? Ask your parents if they kept the receipt. For your brother, not the toy.

🌲 Power cut? Lay unwanted tinsel on the floor to help guide your way around the house, like the lighting they have on the floor of planes.

🌲 Instead of having sprouts as a side dish this Christmas, why not have something tasty instead?

THE OTHER DAYS OF CHRISTMAS

On the first day of Christmas my true love sent to me
A high definition TV.

On the second day of Christmas my true love sent to me
Two turtle doves: it was buy one, get one free.

On the third day of Christmas my true love sent to me
Three French hens, two purple doves
And a game for my PS3.

On the fourth day of Christmas my true love sent to me
Four calling birds, three French beans, a pair of gloves
And FIFA 2012 for Wii.

On the fifth day of Christmas my
    true love sent to me
Five gold rings
They were on eBay by
    half three.

THE XMAS FILES

Name:	Rudolph
Likes:	Joining in other reindeer games
Dislikes:	Having a hooter that's visible from space
Ambition:	To go down in history
Best advice:	Pull together
Favourite memory:	When all the other reindeers shouted "With glee!"

SINGALONGACHRISTMAS

It's beginning to smell a lot like Christmas
Sprout fumes fill the air
The turkey's in the oven
And I'm absolutely lovin'
The whiff of roast potatoes everywhere
It's beginning to smell a lot like Christmas
Just like those ones I've smelt before
It's more than I can handle
Someone light a scented candle
And move Grandma's chair much closer to
    the door.

PIE NEWS

And now the forecast for the Christmas period...

There'll be fog in many areas on Christmas Eve, so if you're out and about on your sleigh, my advice would be to get some help. Overnight there'll be wise men moving in from the East, and any shepherds watching their flocks out there should definitely wrap up warm as temperatures look set to dip below zero.

Excitement levels will continue to rise during the early hours of the morning and there could be a risk of some localised flooding.

Christmas Day should start brightly enough, but after lunch the wind will gradually increase with some gusts reaching as high as 50 miles per hour. As the day goes on an area of high tension will lead to scattered arguments and some fairly major squabbles.

And the outlook for Boxing Day? Mainly overcast with occasional funny periods.

CHRISTMAS TOP TIPS

 Instead of asking what the time is at approximately five-minute intervals the night before Christmas, why not GET A WATCH!!!

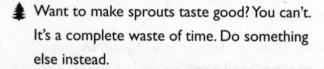 Worried about putting on weight at Christmas? Why not stuff your face with chocolate whilst going for a run?

 Want to make sprouts taste good? You can't. It's a complete waste of time. Do something else instead.

STOCKING FILLERS

We wish you a silly Christmas
And a random new year
I like cheese
Sorry this doesn't rhyme
Or scan properly.

Silent night
It wasn't but
There must've been a power cut.

Chest hair roasting by an
   open fire...
WAKE UP GRANDDAD!!!!!

THE SNOW BALL

Roll up roll up for the Snow Ball
Come dance the night away
Skip the fairy light fantastic
Hip hop hip hop hooray
Roll up roll up for the Snow Ball
It's time to get on down
It just keeps on getting bigger
It's the coolest night in town.

ELEGY FOR A CHRISTMAS TREE

Is there a sadder sight to see

On a rainy day in January

Than a chewed-up, spat-out Christmas tree?

Abandoned, lifeless on the street

Trampled on by passing feet

Unworthy of a second glance

Discarded like a pair of pants.

Dressed to impress you were quite the thing

All spruced up in your tinsel and bling

The king of the castle,
    the lord of the parcel

Fairy-topped and
    tinsel-threaded

Now you're waiting to
    be shredded.

How the mighty
    have fallen

Along with most of
    your needles.

PIE NEWS

Scientists have discovered a link between an increase in global warming in late December and the annual increase in consumption of sprouts over the Christmas period. Said a scientist, "The amount of gas produced is having a direct effect on climate change. In my opinion the only solution is a world-wide ban on sprouts." On hearing the news, children everywhere immediately started celebrating.

CHRISTMAS CROSSES

**What do you get when you cross
a snowman with a vampire?**
Frostbite.

**What do you get when you cross a
sprout with a baked bean?**
Wind.

**What do you get if
you cross a busy
road with a turkey?**
The turkey's eternal gratitude.

**What do you get if you cross
Santa Claus?**
No toys.

BLOW TORCH*

When the match scratched
And the flame came
The snowman
Became a lowman
And then a noman.

* No snowmen were harmed
during the writing of this poem

A SEASONAL REMINDER

Merry Christmas and Happy
    New Year
Let's make one thing
    perfectly clear
Be as nice to your gran as you
    possibly can
It might be the last time you
    see 'er.

SINGALONGACHRISTMAS

Silent night
All is bright
Someone please
Turn off the light.

While shepherds watch their flocks by night
The moon it shines and flickers
One shepherd looks up just in time
To see the angel's knickers.

Away in a manger
No crib for a bed
Should've gone to IKEA instead.

THE XMAS FILES

Name:	Fifi
Job:	Fairy
Age:	Mind your own business
Likes:	Shopping
Dislikes:	Not shopping
Favourite drink:	Fairy liquid
Favourite colour:	Can I go now?
Favourite food:	Seriously. Can I go now?
Favourite word:	Right. That's it. I'm off.

PIE NEWS

A man is being questioned by police on suspicion of not being the real Santa Claus. The man was discovered in a department store earlier today, with a queue of children waiting to see him and tell him what they wanted for Christmas in exchange for a small gift. A number of people dressed as elves are also helping police with their enquiries.

BREAKING NEWS • BREAKING NEWS • BREAKING NEWS

21

IT'S A CRACKING CHRISTMAS FACT...

...that the chances of turkeys taking over the world and wreaking revenge on humankind are actually very slim indeed. Phew!

...that it isn't actually the same robin you see posing on all those Christmas cards. There are many different robins.

...that in some countries the most popular creature featured on Christmas cards isn't a robin at all but a badger.

I'D LIKE TO BE A CHRISTMAS FAIRY

I'd like to be a Christmas fairy
Sitting on a tree
A fairy on a Christmas tree
Is what I'd like to be.

You can keep your Eiffel Tower
And your Himalayas too
A stocking stuffed with sweets and toys
Is what I call a view.

I'd like to be a Christmas fairy
Taking in the sights
The only problem seems to be
That I am scared of heights.

Why couldn't Santa do any gardening?
He'd lost his hoe-hoe-hoe.

Did you hear about Santa trying his hand at stand-up comedy?
He sleighed 'em.

Knock, knock.
Who's there?
Santa.
Santa who?
What do you mean, Santa who? Are you stupid or something?